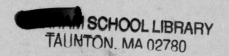

Copyright © 1997 by Nord–Süd Verlag AG, Gossau Zürich, Switzerland.
First published in Switzerland under the title *Hexenfest für Merrilu*.
English translation copyright © 1997 by North–South Books Inc.

First published in the United States, Great Britain, Canada,
Australia, and New Zealand in 1997 by North–South Books,
an imprint of Nord–Süd Verlag AG, Gossau Zürich, Switzerland.

Library of Congress Cataloging–in–Publication Data is available.
A CIP catalogue record for this book is available from The British Library.
ISBN 1–55858–781–0 (trade binding)
1 3 5 7 9 TB 10 8 6 4 2
ISBN 1–55858–782–9 (library binding)
1 3 5 7 9 LB 10 8 6 4 2
Printed in Belgium

For more information about our books, and the authors and artists
who create them, visit our web site: http://www.northsouth.com

Meredith
The Witch Who Wasn't

By Dorothea Lachner

Illustrated by Christa Unzner

Translated by J. Alison James

North–South Books

New York · London

Meredith was a witch who had a broomstick, but often as not she chose to walk.

She knew some spells, but she really liked to make things from scratch.

She loved to sit on the rooftop at sunset, close to the clouds. She made a raucous racket singing bloodcurdling songs with the crows. Meredith was a happy witch except for one thing. She didn't like magic.

Witches have to work on their magic all the time or they might forget the spells. So one afternoon when Meredith wanted a pizza, she decided to try magic–just to keep from getting rusty. Even though she preferred to make her pizza by hand, she forced herself to use a spell: *"Pomodorum shimmy shammy shorum . . . something something korum."* The oven rattled and clattered, smoked and splat–tered. What Meredith took out was burned to a crisp, a smoking circle of soot. Her spell had gone wrong again. Maybe the "something something" part was the problem. Now she was hungry and the kitchen smelled like smoke. She hated magic.

One day Meredith built herself a fantastic house under the stairs. She pretended the house was high in the waving branches of a tree. She was having a wonderful time until the postwitch came with an airmail letter. It was what she had been dreading:

The Annual Assessment of Witchly Powers in Magical Spells
The Last Day of October in the Gathering Green
Spells begin at Midnight
Don't be late!

It wasn't an invitation. It was a command. All the witches would be there, showing off their newly invented spells and their old specialties. There was a test, and anyone who failed would be cast out of the witching society forever. And it was next week!
"Oh, for badness sake!" cried Meredith. "Now I'll have to study spells every day."

But first she had to find her book of magic.
It wasn't in the cupboard and it wasn't under the bed.
It wasn't in the trunk, either. At last Meredith found it
behind the oven. She brushed off the cobwebs and
started to study. She was determined this time to
memorize all the spells correctly.
But when she tried them, they always came out wrong.
Instead of raspberry ice cream, she got ordinary ice
cubes. The cup and saucer disappeared, but didn't come
back. And Meredith nearly turned the cat into a dog!

All too soon it was October thirty–first. Meredith had
no time left. She called to her magic broom, but even it
was being disobedient. Finally she gave up, tucked the
broom under her arm, and started the long walk to the
Gathering Green. It took many hours, but Meredith
enjoyed herself more than she had in a long time. It
felt good to rely on her own two feet to get her where
she was going.

The Gathering Green was aglow with magical light, and witches were arriving with spins and swirls and shrieks of laughter. Nobody noticed Meredith approaching along the road.

"Look at me!" cackled one witch. "No hands!"

"Watch this!" hissed another as she turned a somersault with her broom.

"It makes me dizzy to look," roared Melusina Firebird, the oldest witch of all. "But now, let the spells begin! May I have your attention! The first test is to conjure a fantastic fruit tree."

The air sang with murmurs and whispers. As sudden as lightning, great trees full of luscious, unimaginable fruits appeared. The air was scented with exotic, tropical smells—mango, citrus, papaya, guava, coconut. Meredith remembered the right words to the spell, but what appeared was a tiny apple tree, smaller than herself. One of the witches kindly said, "It's awfully tiny. It will get better with time though, dearie."

"I think it's fantastic already," said Meredith.

"I meant your spell, dear, not the tree."

Before the next test all the witches shared their magical fruit. Meredith tried each kind, but none of them tasted as delicious to her as the fruit from her ordinary trees back home.

The next test was weather: "Conjure a gentle rain and cheerful umbrellas!" instructed Melusina Firebird. Meredith said the spell, but out came hailstones, followed immediately by a bank of fog, and finally a snowstorm. The other witches froze. Quickly they created a rain of cough drops.

A witch consoled Meredith. "You'll have more success with the fireworks," she said.

Wild and wondrous, the fireworks sizzled across the sky.
Meredith gathered her strength and cast her spell. But all
she could conjure was a sparkler, which glittered brightly
for a few minutes, then fizzled out.
"That was very sweet, my dear," said Melusina Firebird.
"But it doesn't pass the test. I'm afraid we can't call you
a certified witch."

At sunrise the witches all mounted their brooms and rode off, but Meredith had to walk home. This time she was tired and her feet were sore. She thought about not being a certified witch any longer, and she thought she ought to feel sad.

When she reached home that evening, she plopped into her rocker, exhausted.

But somehow she just couldn't force herself to feel sad. She kept getting ideas for things that she could do if she didn't have to study spells all the time.

"Bake bread from scratch . . . plant a garden . . . climb a tree . . . build a tree house! That's it! I've *always* wanted to build a tree house!" Completely forgetting that she should be sad, Meredith danced around the room with her cat.

She grabbed a hammer and nails and started building her tree house.

She built it in a tree that had grown slowly, ring upon ring, year after year, until it was steady as the earth and timeless as the moon. The only magic she used was a kiss on her thumb when she accidentally hit it with the hammer.

One night Meredith had a visit from Melusina Firebird and two of her friends. She served them peppermint tea from plants she'd grown, and a cake she'd baked herself.

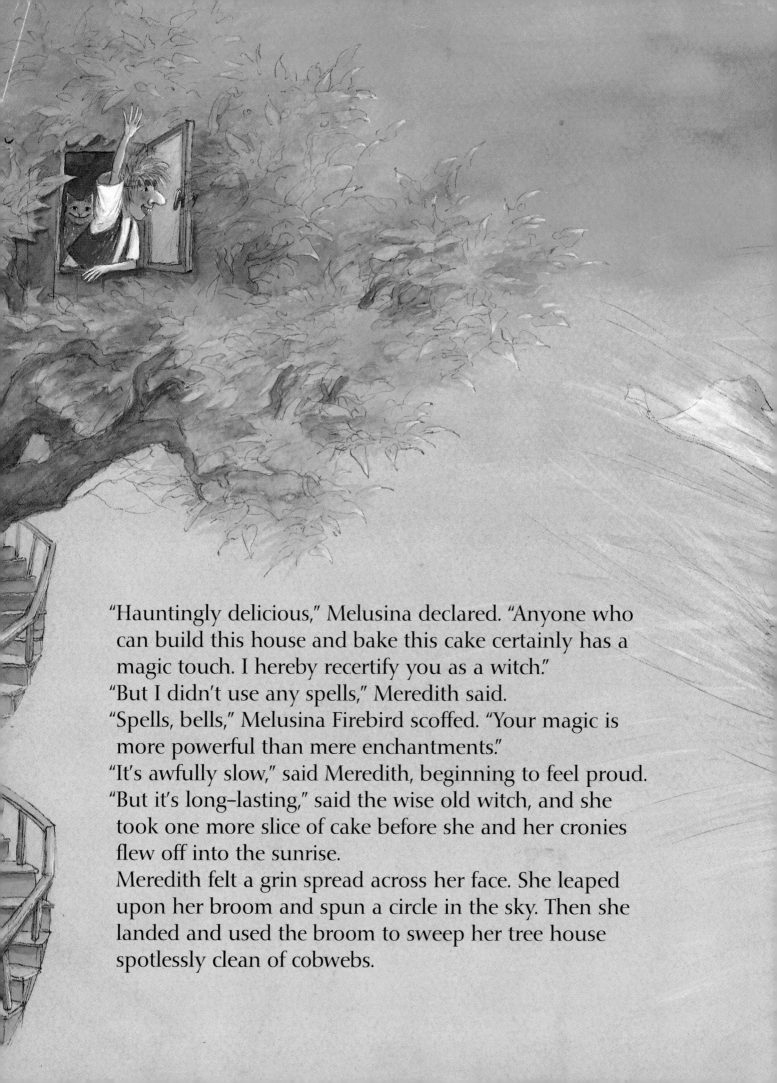

"Hauntingly delicious," Melusina declared. "Anyone who can build this house and bake this cake certainly has a magic touch. I hereby recertify you as a witch."

"But I didn't use any spells," Meredith said.

"Spells, bells," Melusina Firebird scoffed. "Your magic is more powerful than mere enchantments."

"It's awfully slow," said Meredith, beginning to feel proud.

"But it's long–lasting," said the wise old witch, and she took one more slice of cake before she and her cronies flew off into the sunrise.

Meredith felt a grin spread across her face. She leaped upon her broom and spun a circle in the sky. Then she landed and used the broom to sweep her tree house spotlessly clean of cobwebs.

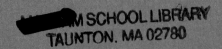